Slam Dunk Series

Gimme an "A!"

Tess Eileen Kindig
Illustrated by Joe VanSeveren

CPH.
SAINT LOUIS

To my friend Diane Walker, the consummate teacher, who laid on my living room floor and let me read a whole book to her. Now THAT's friendship!

Slam Dunk Series

Sixth Man Switch

Spider McGhee and the Hoopla

Zip, Zero, Zilch

Muggsy Makes an Assist

Gimme an "A"!

March Mania

Text copyright © 2000 Tess Eileen Kindig
Illustrations copyrigt © 2000 Concordia Publishing House
Published by Concordia Publishing House
3558 S. Jefferson Avenue, St. Louis, MO 63118-3968
Manufactured in the United States of America

Library of Congress Cataloging-in-Publication Data

Kindig, Tess Eileen.
Gimme an A! / Tess Eileen Kindig.
    p. cm. -- (Slam dunk series)
Summary: While trying to improve his failing math grade in order to stay on the basketball team, Mickey learns a lesson about forgiveness.
  ISBN 0-570-0791-0
[1. Basketball--Fiction. 2. Forgiveness--Fiction. 3. Christian life--Fiction.] I. Tittle.
PZ7.K5663 Gi 2000
   [Fic]--dc21   00-008209

1 2 3 4 5 6 7 8 9 10   09 08 07 06 05 04 03 02 01 00

Contents

Chapter	Page
1. In the Doghouse	6
2. Dealing with the Enemy	14
3. Double Threat—Rivers of Sweat!	22
4. Big-Time Crime	30
5. Muggsy and the Math Munchies	39
6. Brain Flash!	47
7. Another Sight, Another Fright	56
8. Clueless	64
9. Sam's Secret	73
10. A Change of Heart	87

In the Doghouse

"The fans here at Gund Arena are going wild! Nummmmber 11 of the Cavs, Mickey 'Spider' McGhee, has just scored the shot of a lifetime! Folks, you had to see it to believe it!"

The announcer's voice in my head drowned out Mrs. Clay. For at least ten minutes she'd been talking about rectangles. I knew I should be listening, but there's nothing all that interesting about a bunch of boxes. Unless one of them had a brand new basketball uniform inside.

Let me clear something up. I don't really play for the Cleveland Cavaliers. Not yet anyhow. But I *am* a starter for our local rec department team, the Pinecrest Flying Eagles. We're having an amazing season. There's even talk about us making the playoffs. I don't mean to brag or anything, but I'm sort of a superstar. Of course I have to run the treads off my shoes to do it. That's because I'm the shortest guy on the team and the shortest *person* in the entire fourth grade.

"Mickey, would you like to explain how to find

the area of a rectangle?" Mrs. Clay asked. Her voice burrowed into my brain like a mole into a hole.

I looked around. Everybody was staring at me. Including Trish Riley who sits right in front of me. She's a Pinecrest cheerleader and my biggest fan. To Trish Riley, I'm Michael Jordan and Larry Bird all wrapped up in one pint-sized person. If that sounds like bragging, let me tell you right now—it's not! I'd give my Grant Hill basketball card and all the books in my favorite basketball series if it would stop the monster crush she has on me.

"Mickey? We're waiting," Mrs. Clay said, crossing her arms and frowning at me.

"Um, I think you add up all the sides," I answered quickly. As soon as the words hit the air I knew I'd given the wrong answer. *Again*. My best friend Zack Zeno dropped face-down on his desk. That's the thing about Zack. I can always count on him to feel bad for me.

Mrs. Clay sighed. A deep sigh like she was almost too tired to talk. "Michael, you have *not* been paying attention," she said. "Ever since we came back from Christmas vacation it's like you've never rejoined us. I think you'd better see me after class."

A raspberry stain crept up my neck and spilled

across my face. Did I forget to mention that I'm also a world-class blusher? Well, I am. I turn shades of red that haven't even been invented yet. I scrunched down in my seat and hid behind my math book. She'd called me Michael. That could only mean one thing. I was in trouble. *Big* trouble.

"I know! I know!" a voice called out. Sam Sherman's hand flapped in the air. Sam's a Pinecrest starter too. But his real hobby is making my life miserable.

Before Mrs. Clay could call on him, Sam shouted something about multiplying the height by the base. Or half the base. Or something. Whatever it was, he was right. I hate it when he's right. Unfortunately, when it comes to math he's *always* right.

When the bell rang for lunch, everybody mobbed past me. I pretended I was busy cleaning out my desk. I was so hungry I could even have eaten the beanie-weenies on the menu in the lunchroom. If I even *got* to eat, that is. Mrs. Clay was in the front of the room frowning at her grade book.

"Well, Michael," she said when the room emptied. "Perhaps you'd like to tell me what the problem is."

The problem is that I was born without a math

gene. But I didn't dare say a thing like that to Mrs. Clay. She thinks anybody can get math if they try hard enough.

"I guess I'm not trying hard enough," I mumbled, staring at the floor. There was a spot on the carpet shaped like a hermit crab.

"Yes, I can see that," she agreed. She pushed her big, round glasses up on her nose and came over to sit on the edge of the desk next to mine. "What I'd like to know is *why* you aren't trying. Is something bothering you?"

My head snapped up. "No!" I said quickly. "I'm fine. Honest." It was true. I'm the finest I've been in a long time.

"Well then, there must be another reason why you are failing math," she suggested.

"F-f-f-f-f-f-failing?" I asked faintly. The word flew out of the sentence and buzzed around in my brain like an angry hornet. I couldn't believe it. I knew I hadn't been doing great. I never do great in math. But the difference between regular lousy and failing is wider than a regulation b-ball court.

"Yes, failing," she said with another sigh. "I think it's time I talked to your mother."

"No! Please!" I jumped to my feet. This was worse than trouble. This was disaster! If Mrs. Clay called Mom, I'd have the shortest basketball career in the history of the world.

"Yes, I think it's time we got you some help," Mrs. Clay repeated. "You may go on to lunch now. I'll talk with her this evening." She stood up and walked back to the front of the room.

For a second I stood in the aisle wondering what to do. Should I beg? Plead? Promise to do 100 extra problems a night? I already knew it was no use. Mrs. Clay's dialing finger was flexed and ready to call. I shuffled out of the room and down the hall to the lunch room. How long would it take to get to Siberia by bike if I pedaled 12 miles a day, I wondered? But, of course, I didn't know. I was failing math.

"Didn't go so good, huh?" Zack asked as I slid my tray next to his on the table.

"You can say that again," I answered

Zack's eyes bugged out. "Oh man, Mick. You aren't failing, are you? If Coach finds out you're failing, you'll be off the team. Remember what he said that first day of practice? Any guy who fails a class is out. Even if he's a starter."

I'd forgotten that. But Zack was right. Coach *had* said that. And I'd just *made* starter too. Right before Christmas, Tony Anzaldi had fallen off the Christmas tree truck at our fund raiser and hurt his shoulder. Coach had let me fill his spot. Now, not even two months later, I was doomed to be a bench sitter. I shoved my beans around my plate with my fork and thought about Siberia again.

At home my little sister Meggie greeted me at the side door. "Mama's crabby," she warned me. "The dryer went *thunk, thunk, thunk* with all the clothes inside. Then it stopped and a man had to come. It costed lots of money. Seventy-five cents, I think."

She meant $75. Even without a math gene I knew that. In some families $75 might not be a big deal, but in ours it was major. Especially only a month after Christmas.

"Yeah, Mickey," Meggie said. "And guess what made the dryer be broken?"

I didn't have a clue.

"Your scissors!" she shouted. "They were inside a pile of your clothes and Mama didn't see them. The man said they got in behind the drum. Where's the drum in the dryer, Mickey? How come it never plays? I never hear a drum, do you?" She followed me up the stairs, still chattering.

"Hi, Mom," I said as soon as I got into the kitchen. I wondered whether to apologize for the scissors or wait until she told me about them. I decided not to wait. "I'm sorry about the scissors," I added.

Mom was down on the floor with her head in the cupboard under the sink. She took it out and glared at me. "That's what happens when you keep your room looking like a bomb hit it," she snapped.

"I'm sorry," I repeated. "I'll try to clean it up."

She stuck her head back into the cupboard.

My mom doesn't get mad too often. Not this mad anyway. But when she does, the best thing you can do is to leave her alone. I slouched upstairs to my room not even bothering to look for my dog Muggsy. Somehow I had to come up with a plan. A plan that would keep me from being cut from the team.

I wished Zack were home. He's been living at my house since after Thanksgiving when his dad had to take a job with the railroad in Minnesota. Zack doesn't have a mom, so he didn't have anywhere to go except to an aunt and uncle's house in Chicago. But he didn't even know them, so he and his dog Piston came to live with us instead. They'll be here until his dad gets back in April.

Most of the time Zack and I ride home on the bus together. But today he was off at some stupid Photography Club meeting. Zack doesn't know a lens from a shutter. The only reason he signed up is because Shawna Fox is club president. A long time ago we'd agreed we weren't going to like girls until we were at least 27. I kept up my part of the deal. But ever since last Tuesday, Zack hasn't. He's been nuts over Shawna Fox for longer than a whole week. He doesn't think I know. But you'd have to be blind not to see the way he stares at her.

A scream suddenly pierced my thoughts. I jumped up off my bed and raced downstairs.

"What's wrong?" I hollered bursting into the kitchen.

I didn't need an answer. The sleeve of Mom's new pink bathrobe was hanging from Muggsy's teeth. The bathrobe part was nowhere to be seen.

"SOMETHING HAS GOT TO BE DONE ABOUT THAT DOG!" Mom yelled.

Gently, I tugged on the sleeve of Mom's robe. Muggsy growled playfully and ran into the dining room. If things kept up like this, Muggsy and I were going to be spending a lot of time together. In the doghouse.

2

Dealing with the Enemy

After dinner, Zack and I went upstairs to write poems for language arts. His was about snow. Mine was about basketball. It was pretty good too. Except I couldn't think of anything to rhyme with playoffs.

"Coughs ... doffs ... toffs ... loffs," I muttered. I couldn't concentrate. Any minute the phone was going to ring and I still didn't have a plan. Zack and I had tried to make one. But all we'd come up with was trying to convince Mom that basketball and geometry had a lot in common. Round ball. Rectangular court. Diagonal passes. Of course we knew it would never work. If she bought *that*, she'd need more help than I did.

Downstairs in the kitchen the phone shrilled. I stopped muttering. Zack stopped chewing on his pencil. We looked at each other and made a face. This was IT. The call that was going to turn me into a bench sitter.

I shoved back my chair and stood up. Part of

me didn't want to hear Mom talking to Mrs. Clay. But the bigger part had to know whether or not I was benched. "I'll be right back," I said to Zack.

Slowly, I plodded down the steps and into the kitchen. I heard Mom say something about being dismayed. I wasn't exactly sure what dismayed meant. But I knew it wasn't good. Then she said, "I wish we could. I know that would be best. But it's so expensive and right now we can't …" Her voice trailed off.

I could hear Mrs. Clay's voice answering. Only I couldn't make out the words. From across the room she sounded like Charlie Brown's mother on the "Peanuts" specials on TV.

I leaned against the fridge and watched Mom wrap the phone cord around her thumb. She looked at me and frowned. "Yes, that might be best," she said into the phone. "Let's try it. If it doesn't work out, we can go straight to Plan B."

Plan B? They had a Plan B already? This was worse than I thought. I jumped on one foot, then the other. I opened the fridge and closed it again. By the time Mom hung up the phone I looked like I was doing some kind of gorilla dance.

"Well," Mom said when the phone was back on the wall. "That was certainly not good news."

I nodded. At least we agreed about *something*.

Mom crossed her arms and frowned. All she

needed was a pair of big, round glasses and she'd look just like Mrs. Clay. "I think maybe we need to rethink basketball," she said before I could defend myself.

The words hit the air and dropped with a thud onto the kitchen floor. Of course I'd known this was going to happen. But knowing it and hearing it are two totally different things.

"NO! PLEASE!" I practically shouted. "Please, Mom! I'll do anything! Just don't make me quit the team!" I locked my hands together and waved them under her nose. I was begging. Pleading. If she'd let me stay on the team I'd be to math what Bill Gates is to computers.

Mom picked up a sponge and started wiping off the clean counter. For the longest time she didn't say anything. Finally she stopped wiping and turned around. "Okay, Mickey," she said, "You have until Valentine's Day to show me you can do better."

Valentine's Day! That was only two weeks away. How was I going to turn into a math genius in only 14 days?

"B-b-b-but …"

Mom cut me off. "Two weeks, Mickey. That's it. Mrs. Clay wanted me to take you to that new learning center in town, but there's no way we can afford it. So she was kind enough to offer to find you a tutor. If that doesn't work out, you'll have to go to the Title One teacher."

The Title One teacher! My heart sank to my sneakers. Going to the Title One teacher meant leaving class with the other kids who were born without a math gene. People went to Title One for the whole *year*. I plodded back upstairs and sprawled in my chair.

"I have to be tutored," I told Zack. "I have until Valentine's Day to do better, or I'm off the team. Finished. Done. Over. Dead." I punctuated each word with a stab of my pencil. When I was done, my basketball poem looked holier than the knees of my jeans.

The next morning Mrs. Clay cornered me before the bell rang. "Mickey! I have good news for you!" she said in this happy voice she uses whenever she's about to tell me something I won't like. "I spoke with one of your classmates, and he's agreed to stay in at recess and help you get caught up in math."

I looked around the room at the kids squirming in their desks and sharpening their pencils. Who would volunteer to do a thing like that? Zack maybe? But Zack wasn't smart enough to tutor anybody. He just gets by himself with Cs and B-minuses.

"That's right," she said smiling. "Sam Sherman has offered to help you. Isn't that nice? He's got the highest grade in the class. And it looks as if he's trying to be friends."

Mrs. Clay knows that Sam and I don't get along. She's been trying all year to turn us into buddies. But it was never going to work. Sam Sherman only signed up because he thought *tutor* was the same thing as *torture*.

"Do I have to have *him*?" I asked miserably. Title One was starting to look good. Compared to Sam Sherman, Title One was a trip to the amusement park.

"Mrs. Clay, Brittany has a fever," Trish Riley burst in. "Hi, Mickey," she said to me. "She might throw up," she added to Mrs. Clay. "You better come quick."

As soon as she heard the words "throw up," Mrs. Clay forgot about my problems with Sam Sherman. She felt Brittany's forehead and sent her to the school nurse.

I dragged myself over to my desk and sat down. I looked over at Zack, but he was too busy staring at Shawna Fox to care. I wondered what Jesus would do if HE had to be tutored by Sam Sherman. But of course that was a stupid question. Jesus was smart. He'd never need to be tutored. The real question was how would Jesus treat an enemy.

I slumped down in my seat and thought about

it. The answer was as plain as all those Fs next to my name in Mrs. Clay's grade book. Jesus forgave jerks all the time and He wanted me to do the same thing. But could I? Well, maybe. If I didn't have to have one teach me math.

When the bell rang for lunch, Sam Sherman came over to my desk. I was so busy jamming papers inside I didn't see him until he spoke to me.

"Hey, Shrimpo," he said. "Meet me back here as soon as you eat. And make it snappy, okay? My time's valuable."

I gave him my coldest stare. I was wrong about forgiveness. I couldn't forgive Sam Sherman even if he *weren't* my math tutor.

As soon as we shoved our desks together after lunch I knew I was doomed. Right away he gave me the hardest problems in the book. "What's this called?" he demanded, pointing to a long, skinny triangle.

"A wedge?" I asked, uncertainly. It looked exactly like the hunk of wood my dad uses to prop open the door of his basement workshop. Dad calls it a wedge.

"Bzzzzzzzzzzzzzz!" Sam shouted, pressing an imaginary buzzer. "Wrong! I can see we need to go back to the very beginning." He thumbed through the pages of my math book until he came to the easy stuff. So easy even a kindergartner could do it.

"Here, show me what you can do with these," he ordered, pointing to the questions at the end of the chapter.

I bent over the page and scribbled down the answers. While I was writing, Sam tapped his foot on the carpet. "Hey, Shrimpo," he said. "Wanna cut a deal?"

I stopped writing and stared at him. "What kind of deal?" I asked. My scalp felt prickly, like the stick-up hair on top of my head was standing up even straighter than usual.

Sam bent down to tie his shoe that didn't need tying. "Oh, I don't know," he said with his head down by the floor. "I was thinking maybe you won't tell anybody what you saw after Saturday's game if I don't tell Coach you're failing math."

My pencil dropped out of my fingers and rolled off the edge of the desk. I was so amazed I didn't even lean down to pick it up. What had I seen last Saturday? Nothing that I could think of. Zack and I had walked out to the car with my family after the game. We hadn't seen Sam at all except when we drove by him on the way home. What had he been doing then? Just standing on the lawn in front of some broken-down, old house. I scrunched up my forehead and tried to think what could be so bad about that. Nothing came to me.

"Sure," I replied. "No problem."

Sam sat up and flashed me a grin. "Okay, then," he said. "We've got a deal."

"Yeah, we've got a deal," I echoed. I knew I should be happy. I was off the hook with Coach. At least for awhile. But I wasn't happy. I felt uneasy, like I'd just told a lie or stolen somebody's new Jelly Roll pen. And I stayed uneasy for the rest of the afternoon.

On the bus I flopped down on the seat next to Zack. "Remember Saturday when we drove past Sam Sherman in front of that spooky-looking house on Summer Street?" I asked.

Zack shrugged. He was staring at Shawna Fox out the window.

I waved my hand in front of his face and snapped my fingers. "Hey," I shouted. "Knock it off! This is important!"

Zack turned to look at me. "All right, all right. I'm listening," he complained. "We saw Sam by the side of the street. Big deal."

"Do you remember what he was doing?" I asked.

Zack scrunched up his forehead for a second. "Sort of," he said. "He was doing something with a garbage bag. There must have been at least a dozen bags out there. Dark green ones. Why?"

I didn't answer. Suddenly I felt sick. And it wasn't with Brittany's stomach flu.

21

3

Double Threat—
Rivers of Sweat!

"We can win easy," LaMar Watson said as Zack and I walked into the locker room for practice the next night. "The Chatham Cheetahs are no big deal. We've played lots worse than those guys."

The rest of the team agreed. Except for Sam Sherman. "That all depends on who starts for Pinecrest," he said. He opened his locker and pulled out a sweatshirt.

Every player in the room stopped what they were doing and looked at him. Including me.

"What's *that* supposed to mean?" LaMar demanded. "We have our regular starters. Same as always."

"Oh, you never know what could happen," Sam answered, glancing over at me.

A shiver ran down my spine. It was a threat. A reminder that he could get me benched. "I don't think there will be any problem with the starters," I replied, looking him square in the eye.

"I don't think so either," Zack added.

But Sam had scored and he knew I knew it.

Ever since I'd made that stupid deal I couldn't stop wondering what he'd been doing with that garbage bag. His family's rich. Rich guys don't go through people's trash. Especially poor people's trash. Unless, of course, there was something in it they wanted.

"Okay, listen up!" Coach Duffy hollered as soon as we got out on the court. "I've been hearing rumors that some of you guys aren't taking your school work seriously."

My breath caught in my throat. I stared at the floor and prayed my red face wouldn't give me away.

"I don't have names, but I'm putting you all on warning," Coach continued. "Basketball is important, but not as important as school. You can't play in high school or college if your grades are in the basement. And you can't play here either. So let's remember to hit the books, okay?"

I breathed a little easier. He didn't have names. It was just a rumor. But I didn't need two guesses to figure out who'd started it. And why. Sam wanted me to know he was watching my every move. And that he had the power to ruin me. Fear danced on the edge of my nerves. For me, practice was over before it even started. I couldn't have scored if the net had been lowered to my knees.

As soon as Coach let us go, Zack and I made tracks. The cold air was a relief after the heat on the court. As we walked out of the parking lot, I said, "Hey, let's cut down Summer Street, okay?"

"Are you still on that Sam thing?" Zack whined. "I've told you a thousand times it was no big deal. He was just moving a bag out of the way."

"Then why is he so jumpy about it?" I countered. "He's up to something, Zack. I just can't figure out what it is. I bet you anything it's really, really bad too. My F in math is nothing compared to what he's up to."

Zack shrugged. "Okay, let's go take a look. But I don't know what you expect to find."

We crossed the park and turned onto Summer Street. Broken glass crunched under our sneakers as we headed down the sidewalk. The house we were looking for was a tall brick one with lots of sagging porches and a high hedge along the driveway. I knew I'd find it because it's the creepiest one on the whole street.

"Here it is," I whispered to Zack when we were in front of it. I stopped on the cracked sidewalk and stared at the single light shining from an upstairs window. The yellow glow raised goose bumps on my arms. It reminded me of an old show I'd seen on TV once called *The Twilight Zone*.

"What are you whispering for?" Zack demanded. His voice seemed to boom in the quiet street.

"Shhhhhhhhhh!" I snapped, looking around. "You never know who could be hiding."

"Oh, Mick, come on. Get real," he answered, hugging his arms in the cold. "Let's just go home. There's nothing here."

"*Yet*," I said. I grabbed Zack's sleeve and pulled him behind the tall hedge. "Let's just stay here and watch for a second."

"But your mom …" Zack started to protest.

The sound of approaching footsteps cut him off. I yanked his arm hard and we both ducked down low behind the hedge. Through the thick branches we could see someone coming around the side of the house from the alley. Beside me, I heard Zack catch his breath. Even in the gloom we both knew who it was.

Sam Sherman walked past us down the driveway. He was so close we could have reached out and grabbed him by the ankle. Suddenly he stopped. All I'd done is shift my weight a little. I held my breath and clutched Zack's arm tighter. Sam glanced over both shoulders. Then he sprinted up the steep side yard to the path leading to the front door of the house. He put one foot on the bottom step of the porch. Beside me, Zack sniffled.

Sam's foot came off the porch step. He looked over at the hedge. Slowly Zack crept along it on all fours. I followed, being careful not to bump any branches. For once, being the shortest kid in fourth grade was actually a *good* thing.

"Hey!" Sam hollered. "Who's there?"

Zack took off running in a low crouch. I grabbed the bottom of his jacket and ran after him. Behind us we could hear Sam making his way down the steep slope of the yard.

"Go! Hurry!" I croaked at Zack.

Zack straightened up and raced into the alley, dragging me behind him. We ducked behind the house's tilting garage, breathing hard. I poked my head around the corner just in time to see Sam screaming as he wiped mud off his jeans and jacket. He'd slipped on the way down the slope.

"Come on! We've gotta get outta here!" Zack cried, pulling me down the alley.

We didn't stop running until we got to my house. By then we were sweating and out of breath. "Oh ... man, ... Mick," Zack panted. "You ... were ... right! He really is ... up to ... something."

My mind was playing hopscotch. Had Sam been trying to break into that house? If so, for what? And why would he chance it when someone was home? Was he going to steal something outside on the porch? Or had he been planning to hide on the porch and do something else when he was sure the coast was clear? I didn't know. But I knew I had to find out. I opened the side door of my house just as Meggie came clattering down the steps from the kitchen.

"Muggsy made Mama cry," she informed us.

Zack and I looked at each other. How could a *dog* make a grown-up cry? I shrugged out of my jacket, tossed it over a peg by the door, and followed Meggie up to the kitchen. It smelled like beef stew. I took a deep sniff of the warm, spicy scent and felt it warm me up from the inside out. Nothing could be too bad when there was beef stew for supper.

Mom turned from the sink and pointed at Muggsy. He was howling in a wire cage under the table. "THAT DOG," she said, "has gone too far."

I fell to my knees next to the cage. This morning we hadn't even owned a cage. Muggsy let out a series of sharp little yips and stuck both paws through the wire.

"What did you do, buddy?" I asked him. "Did you do something bad?"

"I'll show you what he did," Mom snapped. She banged her stirring spoon down on the stove. "Follow me."

Zack and I trailed her into the dining room. Mom pulled away the edge of the tablecloth and pointed to the leg of the dining room table. Fresh, raw wood made white patches on its fancy claw foot. Muggsy had not only stopped to give the leg a quick chew—he'd tried to have it for lunch!

"*That* is an antique table," Mom said. "It's the only thing I have from my Grandmother Carney. And now look at it!" Tears welled up in her eyes.

Zack and I looked at each other, then back at the table leg. "Wh-where did the cage come from?" I asked.

Boy, you talk about your stupid questions. That was sure a whopper. There's Mom looking like she lost her best friend and all I can think of is the dumb cage.

"I bought it this afternoon at a garage sale," Mom answered, sniffling. "I tried putting him down the basement. But the back of the door will tell you why that didn't work."

Zack and I went to check out the door. Zack opened it and I went down the stairs to see it from the other side. Flakes of white paint dotted the steps. Deep gouges scarred the wood under the doorknob.

"Oh no," I groaned. "This is terrible."

"You can say that again!" Mom said when I came back up. "I'm about at my wit's end,

Mickey. Something has got to be done."

I held my breath and looked at Muggsy's pitiful face behind the wire mesh of the cage. "Like what?" I asked.

"I don't know," Mom said sadly. "But if this keeps up, Muggsy will be needing a new home."

4

Big-Time Crime

Muggsy had a bad case of the munchies. There was no question about it. Last week he chewed up my new Star Wars figure. Jar Jar's snout looks like it had a run-in with a can opener. But as bad as he was acting, he was still only a puppy. He didn't deserve to lose his home. The thought of saying goodbye to Muggsy hurt worse than a toothache.

Zack and I had found Muggsy, Zack's dog, Piston, and Trish Riley's dog, Gabrielle, in the church parking lot last fall. Muggsy had been run over by a car. If we hadn't rushed him to the vet, he would have died. No way could I give him up after all we'd been through together. Besides, I'd waited my whole life for a dog of my own.

"Can't we try to make him stop?" I begged Mom. "Muggsy's part of our family. We can't just give him away."

Mom sighed and went back to stirring the stew. "You're right, Mickey" she said at last. "I just get so upset when he does these things. Of course we wouldn't give him away. But we do have to teach him to keep his teeth to himself."

I breathed a sigh of relief. Somehow God would help me find a way to help my dog. God had sent Muggsy to me and He would help me keep him. I knew it as sure as I knew I was a born basketball player.

The next morning I tapped Trish Riley on the shoulder as soon as I got to school. She turned around in her desk and smiled. "Hi, Mickey. Do you need to borrow a pencil?" she asked.

"No," I answered. "I need to ask you about Gabrielle. Are you having trouble with her chewing on stuff?"

Trish shook her head no. "Gabrielle is a perfect lady," she informed me. "She graduated from obedience school just last week."

"Obedience school?" I asked. "Where's that? Does it cost anything?"

Trish nodded. "It costs $40. They have it at the Y. They're starting a new class pretty soon. Do you want me to find out about it for you, Mickey?" She gave me this weird smile she's been doing lately. She tilts her head to the side and makes her eyes bigger. I guess it's supposed to be cute or something.

"No, that's okay," I muttered.

Obedience school sounded great. Too bad my family didn't have an extra $40 lying around. But

there was no time to think about it right then. I
had too much other stuff to worry about. Like
whether or not Sam Sherman knew it was me and
Zack behind the bushes on Summer Street last
night. I watched him come into the room from
the hall. As soon as he saw me he slammed his
math book down on his desk.

"Okay, Shrimpo," he said from two rows away.
"What's the deal?"

My stomach clenched like a fist. "D-d-d-deal?"
I stuttered.

"Yeah, deal. Did you study what I showed you
last night, or not?"

My breath came out in a gasp. Whew! That was
a close one! It didn't even matter that he'd just
announced to the whole world he was my tutor.
The important thing was he didn't know it was
Zack and me on Summer Street. He must have
fallen down the slope just in time to miss us running toward the back alley. I knew if I had any
sense I'd stay away from Summer Street. But I
couldn't. Already I was planning to go back after
Saturday's game.

I didn't say anything about it to Zack until half-
time. We were leading the Chatham Cheetahs by
ten points. You could practically feel the sparks in
the air as our guys shoved their guys off the paint
to score two three-pointers in a row.

"Are we hot, or what?" Zack cried as we rushed into the locker room.

"It's Pinecrest's game all right!" LaMar agreed, slapping me a high five. "Man, Mick, you were playing mean defense out there."

It's true. I was all over the court. If one of their guys moved so much as a toe, I was right there to stop him. The Cheetahs' coach had already called two timeouts. But all it had done was pump us up even more.

Zack and I collapsed on a bench and uncapped our water bottles. I looked around the room. Sam was talking to Nick Clemmons, the kid who'd first replaced Tony as a starter before Coach picked me. "Hey," I whispered to Zack. "What do you say we go over to Summer Street after this?"

Zack looked at me like I'd fallen on my head. "Are you nuts?" he demanded, loud enough to make Sam look over at us. "After what hap ..."

I glanced over at Sam and shrugged. "Well, that's the way I feel about this game," I said loud-ly. "I don't think we better get too sure of ourselves. They could still win."

For a second Zack looked confused. But he recovered fast and played along. "I keep telling you, we've got it nailed," he said. "Don't you think so, Sam?"

Sam laughed. "When we get done with them,

the Cheetahs will be Chee-*tohs*," he bragged.

It was a great line. I had to give him that. It was also true. We ended up beating them by 15 points, including a terrific three-pointer landed by me. After I nailed the triple, they'd fumbled so bad they couldn't even shoot from the free-throw line.

"Hi, Mickey," Trish Riley called as I walked over to join my parents after the game. "You were awesome today!"

"Thanks," I muttered. I tried to keep going. But she grabbed my sleeve and gave me that big-eyed, head-tilt smile again.

"Do you know what holiday's coming up soon?" she asked.

I knew. I just didn't want to talk about it. "Washington's Birthday," I answered.

Trish laughed. "Oh, Mickey, you're being silly. Of course you know it's almost Valentine's Day. Wait til you see what I have for you."

I could wait a million years. A trillion years. Until the end of the world even. I forced a smile and muttered, "Yeah, well, gotta go."

I spotted Zack standing by the door with my parents and made a beeline for him. "You coming with me?" I asked him. He didn't answer. "Zack and I want to walk home, okay?" I asked Mom.

Mom frowned. "I guess that would be okay,"

she said. "But why would you want to do that? It's awfully cold out there."

"I don't know. I just feel revved up from the game. I need to walk it off," I answered.

Zack still didn't say anything. I leaned on the metal bar that opens the door and started to go out. If he didn't want to go, I'd go by myself.

"Wait," he said finally. "I'm coming."

Meggie wanted to come too. I had to promise we'd play Uno with her when we got home if she'd ride with Mom and Dad. She said okay as long as we played two games and let her be the dealer. We headed out into the cold and crossed over to Summer Street.

"We'd better hurry," I warned Zack. "He might be there already. If he sees us we're dead meat."

Zack picked up the pace. But it was clear he wasn't happy about it. "I don't get it, Mick. This is crazy," he whined. "Why do you want to take a risk like this?"

I didn't know why. I just knew I had to.

At the creepy house we crouched behind the hedge and waited. Just when I thought Sam wasn't coming, we heard the crunch of footsteps heading down the drive from the alley. Sam stopped by the house and looked over both shoulders. Then he darted up the steep slope of the yard. I held my breath and tried not to move a muscle until he was safely on the porch. Through the branches I could see him stop by the front door. His back was to us, but I could see him reaching for something.

Slowly, I inched my head around the side of the hedge for a better look. Sam stuck his hand into the heavy, old, black mailbox next to the front door. He took out some letters. I watched him go through them one by one. When he was done, he pulled a brown envelope out of the stack and stuffed it inside his jacket! Then he rang the doorbell.

I looked at Zack. My eyes were wider than Trish's when she does her head-tilt smile. Zack started to whisper something, but I held my finger to my lips. The front door creaked open. I snuck another peak just in time to see Sam hand the mail to a lady in the doorway. The brown envelope was still stuffed down the front of his jacket.

"Okay, head for the alley, but stay down," I whispered to Zack.

Zack crept along low to the ground and I followed. We didn't talk until we were safely in the alley past the creepy house.

"What did you see?" Zack asked when we reached the corner. "Come on—tell me!"

"Sam stole a piece of mail from the owner's mailbox," I said.

Zack's eyes widened. "Oh, wow. That's a big-time crime."

"You bet it is," I agreed, as we turned onto a short street called Winter Place. "I saw on TV that it's a federal offense to steal somebody's mail. A federal offense is the worst kind of crime there is. They can toss you in jail for that and throw away the key."

"Wow! Do you think we should tell somebody? We probably should," he said, answering his own question. "But if we do, Sam will spill the beans to Coach about your math grade."

I nodded miserably. "I don't know what to do," I admitted. "I need to think about it."

We walked in silence down Winter Place to Wooster Street. Red hearts were popping out on store windows like a bad case of chicken pox. Zack stopped in front of the card shop to look at the valentine display in the window.

"We need to get some of those for the valentine exchange at school," he said. He was pointing at the boxes of cheap valentines kids always give each other. "Don't you think so?"

"Huh? Oh, yeah. I guess," I said dully. How could anybody talk about valentines with a criminal on the loose? Besides, what was so special about Valentine's Day anyhow? As far as I could see, it was just a bunch of mushy stuff.

"Mick?" Zack asked. His eyes shifted from the valentines to the heart-shaped boxes of chocolates. "You know that deal we had about not liking girls til we're 27? Well, I—uh—sort of broke it."

Yeah. I—uh—sort of noticed.

5

Muggsy and the Math Munchies

"Did you decide what we should do about you-know-what?" Zack asked me for the millionth time. Ever since we'd seen Sam steal the mail at the creepy house, Zack had been trying to make *me* decide what we should do about it.

I let out a huge sigh and closed my notebook. I didn't want to talk about Sam Sherman. But even more, I didn't want to measure triangles. It's weird the way the shapes I used to color in kindergarten have all these problems hidden inside them. Who'd have guessed it?

"I don't know, Zack," I said carefully. "Maybe things aren't what they seem. You're always telling me that I jump to the wrong idea about stuff. Remember the Christmas tree sale?"

Zack snorted. "Oh, man, was that funny!"

He dived off his chair and hit the floor with a crash. Just like I did when I got spooked by a customer who turned out to be ... But that's another story. The important thing was I didn't want to risk looking stupid again. Or take a chance on

Sam getting me kicked off the team.

Zack sat up and leaned against my bed. "You know, Mick," he said, "I think if you don't report a crime you're as guilty as the criminal."

His voice was serious. It made my stomach do a flip.

"I know," I agreed. "But what real proof do we have? None. Maybe Sam gave the owner the letter after we took off. We don't know. We need to keep watching for awhile more."

Zack was quiet as he thought it over. Then suddenly he jumped to his feet. I could tell he'd switched gears. Sam Sherman was already history. "Hey, I know what let's do!" he cried. "Let's see if we can get your mom to take us to get valentines!"

I started to pretend-gag, until I looked over at my math notebook. "Yeah, good idea," I agreed. Even valentines were better than math, or Sam Sherman.

Mom agreed to take us as long as we had our homework done. We did. Sort of.

"Okay, then, let's go," she said. She grabbed her car keys off the hook by the basement door. "Meggie can come too."

Zack looked a little freaked by that idea. But I didn't care whether she tagged along or not. It wasn't *me* buying mushy cards for girls.

At the card store we headed straight to the boxes of cheap valentines. Most of the guy ones seemed to have a space theme this year. But Zack and I dug around and found two boxes of basketball cards at the bottom of the bin. Through the clear plastic I could see one that said, "Hoop you have a Slam Dunk day, Valentine!" Personally, I thought they could have skipped the valentine part. But they were the best cards there.

"Is it okay for us both to give out the same kind?" Zack asked.

"Sure," I said. "Who cares? It's a dumb holiday anyway."

Meggie set down a box of Barbie cards and glared at me. "Mickey, that's mean," she said. "Valentine's Day is nice. Isn't it, Mama?"

Mom looked up from a rack of grown-up cards and smiled a weird smile. Sort of like Trish's head-tilt smile. She was holding a card that said, "To My Darling Husband" on the front. It made me squirm just looking at it. I'm glad she likes my dad. I mean, loves him. I really am. I just don't see why she can't do it without the darling thing.

"I—uh—have one more thing to get," Zack said. "I need your help, Mick." He glanced at my mom and his ears turned red. They really did. Usually I'm the blusher, but I saw them. And they were redder than a handful of Red-Hots.

"Meggie and I need to get some candy," Mom said quickly. "We'll meet you guys at the front door after you check out."

"But I want Barbie cards!" Meggie protested.

"Then get them quickly," Mom replied. "I need you to help me pick out candy hearts. The kind you like. The ones with the words on them."

Meggie grabbed the box of Barbie valentines and happily followed Mom to the candy aisle.

"I have money my dad sent me for Christmas," Zack said when they were gone. "So I thought I'd get Shawna one of those nicer cards." He pointed to the rack where Mom had bought the "darling" card.

"You aren't going to get one of those mushy ones, are you?" I asked. "Oh man, Zack. Don't do it. You'll feel like a dope if she shows it to all her friends."

Zack frowned. "I never thought of that," he said. "Well, okay, but let's at least look." He walked over to the rack of cards and I followed. I just hoped we wouldn't see anyone we knew.

"Get a funny one," I urged him. "Like this." I handed him a card with two ducks on the front. One was flapping its wings and jumping up in the air over a heart-shaped puddle. The other one was laughing. Inside it said, "You quack me up, Valentine!"

Zack read it and groaned. He picked up a card with pink hearts on the front.

This was boring. I yawned and wandered away. Up at the front of the store I could see Mom and Meggie paying for the "darling" card, the Barbie cards, and the candy hearts. I wandered over to the candy aisle to see if they had any new Pez dispensers.

"Should I get the yellow one or the red? Which do you think she'd like?" a familiar voice asked.

I froze in my tracks. The voice was coming from the other side of the rack where the expensive candy was shelved. I was looking on the cheap side.

"Either one is fine, Sam," a cranky voice replied. "But please hurry up and choose. I have to be at the library board meeting in 15 minutes. And I still have to drop you at home."

It was Sam's mother. Sam Sherman was buying valentine candy. For a girl. Who wasn't his mom. I couldn't believe it. Sam Sherman didn't like girls. Sam Sherman didn't like anybody. Except Sam Sherman. Who would he be buying chocolates for?

A slow grin crept over my face. Poor Sam. He needed help deciding. I was a good decider. It was the least I could do to help him after he'd helped me with math. I walked around the candy aisle.

"Get the yellow one," I advised.

Sam jumped a foot. "Let's get outta here," he mumbled to his mom. They left without getting either the yellow *or* the red. I stood in the candy aisle grinning.

When they were gone, I hightailed it over to Zack. "Did you see who was here?" I asked him. I didn't give him time to answer. "Sam Sherman! And he was buying candy. For a girl! Who could it be?"

Zack looked up from the card he was reading. This one had *lace* on it. "Sam doesn't like girls," he said. "No way."

"Well, I saw him," I insisted.

Zack didn't answer. He put back the lace card and picked up a plain one with two kittens on the front. "Okay, I'm ready," he said.

I grinned at him. "Can I see it?" I asked, pointing at the card.

Zack handed it over. Two kittens sat on either side of a red heart. On the heart it said, "It's Valentine's Day." Inside, plain black letters like a kid's printing read, "Hope yours is purrrrrr-fect!"

I handed it back and held up both thumbs. "Good job, buddy," I told him. I meant it too. The card wasn't mushy, but it was still girlie. Shawna would know he liked her because it was bigger than ordinary valentines. It was a stroke of genius!

Zack grinned. "Yeah, this'll work," he mumbled.

All the way home we tried guessing who Sam might have been buying candy for.

"You don't suppose it's Trish Riley, do you?" Zack asked. "He did invite her to his birthday party, remember?"

I remembered. That was the night I got short-shirted by the Harlem Globetrotters. It was one of the best nights of my whole life—even though Zack got invited to Sam's party and I didn't. "Nah," I said. "It's not Trish. No way." But what if it was? Did I care? No way!

"Probably not," Zack agreed. "I guess we'll have to wait and find out."

"Well, I think it's very sweet of him," Mom said from the front seat. "I know Sam isn't your favorite guy. But I think this goes to show you that everybody has some good in him if you look deep enough."

"Sam? *Good?*" I squawked. "Mom, you don't KNOW this guy!"

"That's right, Mrs. McGhee," Zack added. "He's as mean as a snake."

Mom shook her head as she turned into our driveway. "It may seem that way sometimes," she said. "But I think it's lovely that he's trying to make somebody's holiday special. God wants us to look for the good in everybody, guys. Even the people who do things we don't like. Sometimes it's hard to understand why they do what they do, but God helps us see past the bad stuff. That's what forgiveness is all about."

She pulled up to the side door of the house and stopped the car. "Okay, out you go. I'm going to put the car in the garage and I expect you all upstairs when I get done."

We piled out of the car and into the house. Dad had fallen asleep in his recliner in the living room. When he heard us come in, his eyes popped open. "I'm just watching the game," he said. A bunch of people in khaki pants were line-dancing across the screen.

"Sure, Dad," I teased. "Who's winning?"

Dad gave us a sheepish grin. "Okay, busted," he agreed. "I've been asleep most of the third quarter."

We laughed and went upstairs to my room. "He does that all the time," I told Zack. "Whenever we aren't around to ..." Something on the stairs caught my eye. "What's this?" I asked, picking it up.

"I don't know," Zack answered. "But there's another one. And another one. And another ..."

"YEOWWWWWWWWWW!" I bellowed. "It's my math notebook! Muggsy ate my math notebook!"

6

Brain Flash!

"Where's your math notebook, Mickey?" Mrs. Clay asked.

I swallowed hard. "M-m-m-m-my dog ate it," I stuttered. My face felt redder and hotter than Texas chili.

The whole class cracked up. Except for Mrs. Clay. She crossed her arms and frowned at me. "Michael, that is the oldest excuse in the book," she snapped. "If you didn't do your work, at least try to come up with something better than that."

"But it's true," I said miserably. "Look." I reached into my desk and pulled out a brown paper bag. Twenty-six pairs of eyes watched as I dumped it out. Jagged scraps of torn paper scattered across my desk and fluttered to the floor. The wire that had held the pages together fell with a plop on top. I held it up to Mrs. Clay. It looked like Trish Riley's hair after her mother uses the curling iron on it. *Sproinnnnnngggggg!*

Mrs. Clay stared at the mess on my desk. Her mouth twitched. She was trying hard not laugh, but a snorty little giggle popped out of her lips. "Mickey," she said. "You're the only kid I've ever taught who got away with that one!"

Wild clapping broke out all over the room. I looked around. Even Sam Sherman was beating his hands together! I was stunned. Speechless. Trish turned around in her seat. "You're so cuuu-uuuuuuute, Mickey!" she squealed.

"You still have to do your math though," Mrs. Clay warned, sounding like herself again. "I'll expect last night's work and tonight's completed by tomorrow."

"I'll have it," I promised. So what if I had double the homework? The whole class had clapped for me! Of course Trish had said that dumb thing. But then she says dumb things a lot.

Mrs. Clay began talking about the long skinny triangles that look like wedges. Since I now know they're called scalene triangles, I decided to think about Muggsy. Mom was right. Muggsy had the worst case of the munchies in the world. Maybe even in the universe. He needed obedience school like a hot dog needs mustard. But it was out of the question.

I had to help him myself. Only how? I didn't even know why he chewed stuff. He has a rubber mouse that squeaks, a rawhide bone, and a hard rubber ball. But he'd rather chew on bathrobes, table legs, and math notebooks. Did they taste better? If they did, Zack's dog, Piston, was sure missing out on an awful lot of treats.

A strange noise scraped across my thoughts. Trish's friend Brittany was filing her nails with one of those scratchy brown files. I imagined what it would be like to chew on *that*. It made my teeth feel so weird I almost yelped out loud.

"This is not a beauty parlor, Brittany," Mrs. Clay said. "Put the file away or it's mine."

Brittany stuck the file in her desk and yawned. *Ding! Ding! Ding! Brain flash!* Brittany was doing what she wasn't supposed to do because she was bored. Was it possible that Muggsy broke the rules because he was bored too? Maybe all Muggsy needed was something new and exciting. A fantastic idea dropped into my brain ready-made.

After school I raced into the house and up the stairs to the kitchen. "Mom! Mom!" I hollered. "I'm taking Muggsy to basketball practice, okay?"

Mom looked up from the counter where she was chopping carrots. "Well, hello to you too!" she said. "What's this about Muggsy?"

I was so hyped I could hardly talk. "I think he needs to get out more," I explained. "He's bored. If he has more fun he'll be tired when he's home and won't chew up our stuff."

Mom laughed. "If Coach won't mind, it's fine with me. I could use the break. He chewed open a bag of onions this afternoon. There are onion skins all over the house, including the bathroom! He's in the cage at the moment. In your room."

I raced upstairs and freed Muggsy from his doggie prison. Then I grabbed my gym bag and his leash, and tore back down. Zack was coming to the rec center straight from school. He'd had to go to a short meeting of the Shawna Fox—I mean the *Photography*—Club. So Muggsy and I were on our own. We trotted off down Arvin Avenue like we went places together every day.

At first it was fun. Until a Great Dane showed up. Muggsy growled and charged at the dog's kneecaps. I had to yank his leash and cross the street or he'd have been dog soup. After that, he went crazy. By the time we got to Pinecrest Park I was panting from just trying to keep up.

Zack was already in the locker room when Muggsy and I burst in. "Whoa! What's he doing here?" he asked as the guys gathered around my dog. "Does Coach know?"

"Nope," I answered. "But he won't care. Muggsy needs some fun."

"Whoof!" Muggsy agreed. He strained at his leash and took a sharp right. The leash wrapped around my ankles.

"Stop it!" I hollered as he used my ankles for a maypole again.

"Mugg-seeeee!" I yelped as he did it again.

I took a step and toppled over like a tower of blocks. The team hooted.

I unwound the cord from my ankles and struggled to my feet. Muggsy licked my red face and wagged his tail. This time I was in no mood to make up. I tied the end of the leash to my locker handle and got ready for practice fast. I knew I had to talk to Coach before everybody got out on the floor. Suddenly I wasn't sure Coach was going to find my idea so wonderful. Suddenly I wasn't so sure I found it all that wonderful myself.

Coach Duffy was standing on the edge of the court looking over some notes. I came up behind him with Muggsy. "Uh, Coach?" I asked.

He turned around and saw Muggsy. "What's that dog doing here? And don't tell me you're babysitting," he barked.

I knew he was thinking about the time Zack and I were babysitting Dulcie, the little girl across the street. We'd had to bring her to practice. It's a long story, but we'd all wound up going home in a police car. "No, no babysitting," I said quickly. "This is my dog, Muggsy. He just needed an outing. I'll tie him to the pole over there and he'll be fine. He might bark some, but it's only because he loves basketball. It gets him excited."

Coach frowned. Muggsy wagged his tail. Coach sighed. Muggsy wagged harder. "Okay," Coach said finally. "But I don't want this to become a regular thing, you hear?"

"It won't," I promised.

I tied Muggsy to the pole and joined the starters on the floor. Luis Ramez and LaMar were battling each other for the ball. I grabbed a ball of my own and dribbled over to Zack.

"Come on, let's do a little one-on-one to warm up," I said.

I dribbled toward the paint, aimed, and shot over Zack's flailing arms. A miss. Both of us ran for the rebound. Zack snatched it. He held the ball against his chest, teasing me with it. Then he let it fly. Another miss. I stormed in after it, but Zack was already there. He grabbed it, pivoted to the right, and landed a sinker.

Coach Duffy blew his whistle. "Okay, guys, listen up!" he hollered. "Mickey and Zack just showed us something we need to talk about. Offensive rebounding is a skill you could all stand to improve. Height helps, but it's not everything. Mickey, part of why Zack beat you out is because you waited too long to go after the ball."

Waited too long? What did he mean waited too long? I'd crashed in there like a madman. I opened my mouth to protest, but Coach ignored me.

"You can't stand around watching the flight of the ball," he explained. "It may only be a second, but you don't HAVE a second. The best thing you can do is expect every shot to miss."

"Whaaaaat?" I squawked. This didn't sound like Coach Duffy. He was always telling us to be positive.

"That's right," he said. "If you expect the shot to miss you're going to position yourself for the rebound. And position is everything. I don't care if you're a giant. If you aren't in position, you aren't going to get the ball. It's as simple as that. Mickey and Zack, give us some more one-on-one."

The rest of the team stood back and let us own the floor. Zack took control of the ball and started dribbling towards the paint. He aimed, shot, and missed. Both of us lunged for the rebound. I claimed it. Nailed it. A nice two-pointer!

Coach blew his whistle again. "Good, Mickey," he said. "You were faster that time. Zack, you have to think where the ball is going to land. You expected it to bounce back to you. But most of the time it's not going to. Bounce-backs only happen when you shoot from straight in front of the hoop. Shots taken from the side usually bounce to the opposite side."

This was cool stuff. I really felt myself getting into it. I'd never thought about there being a way to tell where the ball might land. From then on, I played like a whirling windstorm. Every time the action heated up, Muggsy barked and ran back and forth on his leash. But I was too into what I was doing to enjoy watching him. When Coach blew his whistle to end practice it felt like only ten minutes had gone by. I was hot, sweaty, and jazzed.

"Hey, Mick," Zack called. "Slow down a sec."

I had been jogging off to the locker room, but I stopped and turned around. "I want to hurry and get home. What's so important?" I asked.

Zack let Sam, Luis, and LaMar pass before he answered. "I think I know who Sam was buying the candy for," he whispered. "Brittany. I saw him talking to her after school."

I shrugged. Who cared who Sam gave candy to? All I wanted to do was work on my rebounding skills some more. "Wanna shoot some more hoops when we get home?" I asked. "The snow's almost melted."

"Sure," Zack answered. "We can let Muggsy and Piston run around. So, do you think Sam likes Brittany?"

I ignored the question and looked over at

Muggsy. My idea had worked! Muggsy had had fun watching us play. And now he was lying down quietly with his back to the court. I walked over to him, "Hey, Muggs," I called, "Good job, buddy."

At the sound of my voice, he jumped up on all fours and turned around.

I stared. Muggsy stared back. The handle of Coach's gym bag was hanging out of his mouth. The gym bag was nowhere to be seen.

7

Another Sight, Another Fright

Saturday's game against the Strongsville Sabers was an away game. I hate away games for two reasons:

1. You aren't on your own turf, and
2. Most of the crowd hopes you mess up.

It looked like the screaming people in the stands were going to get their wish. At the start of the second half we were down six points. I just couldn't seem to get my act together. It wasn't that I was playing terrible. It's just that I wasn't playing great.

But then, with only ten minutes left on the clock, something weird happened.

Brittany, who is head cheerleader, started what the guys on the team call the Show-Off Cheer. The way it works is she hollers a question to each of the cheerleaders one at a time. And one at a time they all holler back the same answer. The whole idea is for each girl to show off her best jump or flip.

"HEY, HEY, LISA! WHADDA YA SAY?" Brittany screamed to Lisa Adamson.

Lisa did a cartwheel and answered, "HEY, HEY, PINECREST! TAKE IT AWAY!"

"HEY, HEY, BONNIE! WHADDA YA SAY?" Brittany bellowed next.

"HEY, HEY, PINECREST! TAKE IT AWAY!" Bonnie Freeman yelled and did a back flip.

"HEY, HEY, TRISH! WHADDA YA SAY?" Brittany screamed.

Trish Riley jumped out of line and landed in the splits. "HEY, HEY, MICKEY! TAKE IT AWAY!" she shouted.

"Did you hear that, folks?" the announcer boomed before Brittany could get to Joy Rankin. "That was a little moral support for Nummmmmmmber 11 of the Pinecrest Flying Eagles, Mickey 'Spider' McGheeeeeeeeeeeee!"

The sound of my name flipped my "go" switch. Not when Trish said it, but when the announcer said it. Suddenly I was scooping up rebounds like peanuts. By the time we walked off the floor with the win, I was wired. Enough to visit Summer Street again.

As soon as we got home, Zack and I gulped down a peanut butter sandwich, an apple, and a handful of carrot sticks and took off. We had some trouble getting away from Meggie. We had to promise to let her play "hooky" when we got back. That's what she calls messing around with Zack's table hockey game—playing hooky. We've told her a thousand times it's *hockey*, but she always forgets.

"Maybe we're too late," Zack said as we turned down Summer Street. His voice sounded hopeful.

I knew how he felt. Part of me didn't want to see anything bad either. I had a killer math test coming up on Monday that needed every bit of brain power I had. If I passed, I'd be off the hook with Mom and Mrs. Clay. And *on* the basketball team.

"I don't see how we could be late," I replied. "Sam was in Strongsville just like us. I heard him tell Luis he was going to McDonald's for lunch. We're probably early."

Zack didn't answer. We'd reached the creepy house. Both of us knew we needed to stay alert. If Sam saw us skulking around in the bushes, he'd rat on me to Coach Duffy for sure. The house looked all closed up. Every window was covered with shades. Maybe nobody was there. For half a second I almost decided to give up and go home. Then my brain flashed a picture of Sam stuffing the brown envelope down the front of his jacket.

"Come on," I said to Zack. "Let's stake out over there." I pointed to the bushes.

Zack sighed. He followed me to what was becoming our regular hiding place. We crouched down and waited. I wished we could sit on the ground, but it was way too cold. Minutes passed. My ankles started hurting. More minutes passed. I think my nose froze.

"This is stupid," Zack said after still *more* time went by. "Let's go."

"No," I said. "He's coming. I know it."

More minutes went by. He didn't come.

"Okay, that's it," Zack said, standing up. "I'm outta here."

"No! Wait!" I jumped up too, then quickly ducked back down. "I know he's coming, Zack! I know it. We just have to have patience."

"I don't want to have patience," Zack replied. "I want to have a mug of hot cocoa. I'll see you later, Mick."

Zack stuffed both hands into the pockets of his jacket and took off toward Arvin Avenue. He didn't even look back to see if I was following. For a second I thought about running after him. But I couldn't. It was like my feet were frozen to Summer Street.

I don't know how long I waited, but it must have been at least an hour. Cars went by in an endless parade. Two dogs sniffed me. An old lady asked me what I was doing. I said, "Looking for something." Which was sort of true. Finally though, even *I* got the picture. Sam wasn't coming.

I stood up and stretched. All I wanted to do was get home and get warm. The fastest way to get there was through the alley that ran along the back of the house. It's a good shortcut. I normally don't take it though, because it means crossing people's yards. But I was freezing and I'd already *been* in somebody's yard for most of the afternoon. I followed the line of bushes to the back, staying on the side farthest away from the creepy house.

Crack!

The sudden sound of breaking glass brought me to a fast stop. A shiver of fear crawled down my spine like an ugly bug. Carefully, I peered through the thick branches of the hedge to the back porch of the house. An old trellis covered with thick vines blocked my view, but I could see something moving. It was the exact color of Sam's black and red jacket. He had just broken a back window of the house! I pulled back the branches and watched. Carefully, he reached in through the opening and pulled off the jagged pieces of broken glass that hadn't fallen onto the porch. I opened my mouth to yell at him. No words came out. I was frozen. Like a snowboy who could only stand in the yard and stare.

Sam hoisted his leg over the window sill and ducked his head in the house. "Hello!" he hollered. "Anybody home?"

There was no answer. I watched as his other leg went over the windowsill. For a second I could hear his voice inside the house still calling. The only sound after that was the *slick, swish* of tires on the wet street.

I didn't know what to do. I could knock on the door. I could run for help. I could stick around and see what happened next. Or I could get out of there and go where it was safe. My feet decided for me. I took off toward the alley at a dead run and didn't stop until I was home.

God wants us to look for the good in everybody, guys. That's what Mom had said the night we went to get valentines. But why would God expect to me find good in a person who stole mail and broke into houses? How could there be any good in somebody like that? I didn't know. All I knew is that I needed to talk to Zack. Now.

"Hi, Mom. Gotta go talk to Zack," I cried, storming through the kitchen.

Mom looked up from the pan of brownies she was taking out of the oven. "What? Mickey McGhee running past brownies? Wow. There's a first," she teased.

I didn't answer. I took the steps two at a time and practically fell in a heap at the top. "Zack! Zack!" I called as I ran toward my room.

The door was partway open. Zack was lying on his bed reading a basketball book from the series we both like. He raised up on one elbow and gaped at me as I flew through the door.

"What's the matter with you?" he demanded. "You look like you've seen a ghost."

"I've seen—something—worse," I said, gasping for breath.

My wild eyes made Zack close his book. He sat up and swung both legs over the side of the bed. "What's the matter, man?" he asked. His eyes were as big as the bottoms of two brown bottles. "What happened?"

The story spilled out in a rush. "Now what do we do?" I asked when I was done.

Zack shook his head. "Oh man, Mick, I don't know. If we tell your parents or Coach, it's all over for Sam. And maybe for you too. He'll tell about your math grade just to get even. But ..."

I knew what he was going to say before he said it. We couldn't keep something this big a secret.

"We have to tell," I said. "We *have* to. Even if it means my not getting to play anymore."

Trust me—that sounded a whole lot braver than it was. I felt so sorry for myself I wanted to go to bed and pull the covers over my head. It was so unfair. I'd been working hard with Sam. I'd learned a whole lot about math. Maybe not everything, but a lot. And now it wasn't going to matter. I was still going to get kicked off the team.

"Let's go down and talk to your Mom," Zack urged me.

I shook my head. "No. Not Mom. Not yet," I said. "She'll get all worked up and call Sam's parents. Or the police. I don't know, Zack. What if I'm wrong? What if there's some explanation for it all?"

Zack shook his head like he could hardly believe what he was hearing. "You just don't want to tell," he accused me.

"No, I don't," I agreed. "But I said I'm going to. And I am."

"So who are you going to tell then?" he demanded.

The word dropped into the space between us as neatly as a b-ball in the hoop. "Sam," I replied.

8

Clueless

The phone was ringing as we came in the door from church the next day.

"I'll get it!" Meggie screeched, tearing past me and up the stairs. The kid's like Superman. She hears a phone and she'd leap a burning building in a single bound to get to it.

"Miiiiiikkkkkeeee! IT'S FOR YOU!" she hollered. "Some boy. Not a very nice one either," she whispered as I came into the kitchen.

Two guesses who that was. My heart pounded as I took the receiver and said hello.

"Hey, Shrimpo," said the voice I expected. "I'm in a good mood today. I've decided to do you a little favor."

"Wh-what kind of favor?" I stammered.

Zack was taking off his jacket in the kitchen. He stopped and raised his eyebrows.

"I thought I'd help you study," Sam Sherman offered. "The unit test in math is tomorrow in case you forgot. From what I've seen, you need all the help you can get, pal."

He'd get no argument there. I still didn't know an octagon from a hexagon. But seeing him today meant I had to talk to him today. And I wasn't sure I was ready for that.

"What's the catch?" I asked, stalling for time.

"No catch," Sam answered. "I just thought I'd be nice. But if you don't want to, that's fine with me."

My mind waged a five-second war with itself. I didn't want to talk to Sam about what I'd seen. But even more, I didn't want to fail math. There was no contest. "I want to. I want to," I said quickly. "I'm just kinda surprised *you* want to. Where do you want to meet? You can come over here."

"No way," Sam replied. "I'm not *that* nice. You come here. 3:00." He hung up the phone before I could answer.

"I have to go to Sam's for tutoring," I announced as I hung up the phone.

"Oh, man," Zack muttered.

"Oh, wonderful!" Mom exclaimed. She was at the counter already making baloney sandwiches for lunch. "See, Mickey, it's just like I told you. There's good in everyone if you look hard enough."

Zack and I exchanged glances. Well, *almost* everyone, we agreed silently.

By the time I got to Sam's house my throat felt like I'd swallowed a gym sock. I'd had a terrible thought while I was standing on the corner of Wooster Street waiting for the light to change. Maybe Sam's offer to help me study was just another one of his deals. Maybe he'd seen me out the window of the creepy house and was just trying to keep me quiet. If that were the case, I could forget about getting any extra help. He'd try to cut me a deal the second I got there. And when I refused, he'd kick me and my math book out into the street.

I rang the bell wishing I'd said I was busy. Nobody answered. Just as I about to ring it again, Sam pulled open the heavy oak door.

"You're here," he said in a flat voice. "Come on in." He sure didn't sound thrilled to see me.

I followed him into the foyer. The house was so quiet all you could hear was the sound of the furnace breathing in the basement. Streams of colored light from the stained glass window on the landing painted the floor with red and gold stripes. It felt like being inside a church.

"Where should we study?" I asked.

Sam laughed. "What are you whispering for?"

"I don't know," I said in my regular voice. "It's just so quiet here. Where is everybody?"

"Not home," Sam said matter-of-factly. "Come

on back to the kitchen."

Sam and I were alone in the big silent house. The hair on the back of my neck stood up straighter than the stick-up hair on top of my head.

I said a quick prayer and followed him into a big bright room with a floor like a giant black and white checkerboard. Copper pots hung from the ceiling. Plants crowded the ledge of a bay window by the table. The fridge was covered with wood and built into the wall. But what caught my eye were the little squares of yellow paper stuck to everything. The one on the microwave said:

> Punch holes in plastic of
> frozen dinner before heating.

Sam saw me reading it and yanked it off the microwave door. "My mother," he explained. "She doesn't think I can remember anything. I take care of myself all the time."

I didn't know what to say. My mother hardly ever leaves me notes because she's almost always there when I get home. And she never leaves me frozen dinners. Though it might be cool if she did. Once in awhile anyway.

Sam reached into the built-in fridge and took

out two cans of soda. He flipped the tops and set them on the table. "We can work in here," he said. "Sit down."

I sank into a chair and shrugged out of my jacket. No way could I say anything about what I'd seen. Not with Sam and me alone in the big house. Sam could get mean. I'd never really seen him do anything, but twice I'd seen him get this look. It curled my toes just thinking about it.

Sam opened my math book and pointed to a figure. "What's that called?" he asked.

I didn't know. But I breathed a sigh of relief. He hadn't seen me out the window after all! The offer to help me wasn't a bribe. I settled down and got to work. We worked through two cans of soda each and a whole bag of barbecued potato chips. We worked so long that when I looked up at the window it was dark outside. I hadn't even noticed Sam flip the light on.

"Yikes! What time is it?" I asked.

"5:30," Sam replied, glancing at the clock on the microwave.

"I need to call home and get somebody to come pick me up," I said. I looked around the big kitchen for a phone. "Your parents will probably be home pretty soon, huh?"

Sam shrugged. "Not til 7:00," he said. "That's why there was the note on the microwave. They went to some party thing at the art museum. I don't mind. I'm used to it."

I wondered what it would be like to be all alone in your house at night. I'd hardly ever been alone in my house in the daytime. I gathered up my papers and math book and stuffed them into my backpack. Then I found the phone and called home.

As usual, Meggie answered on the first ring. "Hi, Mickey," she greeted me. "We made clown faces. Guess what with?"

"I don't know, Meg. Let me talk to Mom, okay?"

"I can't," she replied. "Mama has company. Dulcie's mother is here. Mama said, 'If that's for me I'll have to call back.'"

"Then let me talk to Dad," I said.

"I can't," Meggie answered. "We made clown faces with pears. We put the pears on the lettuce and then we stuck on raisins for eyes and then ..."

"Meggie, let me talk to Dad," I said, clenching my teeth. I looked over at Sam. He was playing with a Game Boy, but I could see him smirking.

"I can't," Meggie replied. "You didn't listen to me, Mickey. I said I can't. Daddy is taking a shower. He got dirt on him from the basement."

"What? Oh, never mind," I growled. "Just let me talk to Zack then."

Meggie sighed. "I can't. Zack is sleeping. Mama thinks he's getting a cold. Guess what we used for noses? Guess!"

"Meggie," I said trying to sound patient. "Will you please tell somebody I need a ride home? Now!"

There was no answer.

"Meggie?" I asked sternly. "Are you nodding your head? Remember how I told you that does not work on the phone?"

Sam let out a huge snort of laughter. I turned my back to him. "Meggie, tell someone to come get me. Say yes if you heard me and are going to do that."

"Yes, Mickey," she replied. "But, Mickey, you didn't guess what we used for noses."

"Cherries," I said wearily. "It's always cherries for noses."

Sam cackled. I hung up the phone and shrugged. "Little sisters!" I sighed. "What a pain!" But I knew my face was redder than the clown noses on those canned pears.

Sam went back to his Game Boy and I stood by the counter watching him. It felt like two hours went by. Now that we were done working on math, there wasn't anything to talk about. Except IT. And I wasn't ready to talk about IT yet. Finally I said the only thing I could think of.

"So, whatcha been up to lately?"

Sam's head jerked up from his Game Boy. "What's that supposed to mean?" he demanded.

"Nothing," I said, looking out the kitchen window. I wondered how long it would take for one of my parents to drive the six blocks to get me.

"That's my answer too," Sam replied. "Nothing. I've been doing nothing."

I stared out the window into the kitchen of the house next door. A man was standing on a ladder painting the walls. For a second I watched his arm go up and down, up and down. I thought about what I'd seen on Summer Street and how Zack said I was guilty too if I didn't tell. I also thought about what Mom had said about everyone having some good inside them and God expecting us to find it.

"Sam?" I asked.

"What?" This time he didn't look up from his game.

"I saw you break the window of that house on Summer Street." I don't know why I said it. I hadn't planned to. The words just came out. It was so strange. It was like I was watching the man paint and watching myself talk to Sam at the same time. "I saw you steal the lady's mail too," I added.

"Oh yeah?" Sam sneered.

I could see his reflection in the window glass. He put down the Game Boy and glared at me.

"You think you know it all," he snarled. "But guess what? You don't know anything. You're clueless, pal."

9

Sam's Secret

"What do you think he meant?" Zack asked later that night when we went to bed.

"I don't know. That's why I think he might be right. I *am* clueless!" I moaned.

"Baloney!" Zack said loudly. He sat up in his bunk. "Sam just didn't want to admit we caught him. We gotta tell your mom for sure now."

I was silent for awhile thinking it over. I knew Zack was right. But I also knew something else. I had to give Sam another chance. If there were any good in him at all, I had to try and find it. I'd give myself one more try. If I didn't find out the truth I would tell my parents on Valentine's Day night.

I sighed, thinking about the next day. I wished I could start the week on Tuesday. Monday meant a double whammy of bad things—Sam and the killer math test.

The next morning I got to school with two brand new yellow pencils and a headful of math facts. Hexagons had six sides. Octagons had eight. I was as ready as I'd ever be to prove my stuff.

Mrs. Clay passed out the test. I looked mine over. No sweat. I could do it with my hands tied behind my back. I grinned at Zack and turned the paper over. On second thought, maybe there would be sweat after all. Streams. Rivers. Lakes. Maybe even oceans of it. There was stuff on this test I'd never seen before!

"Ready?" Mrs. Clay asked, glancing at the clock. "Okay, begin."

I grabbed my yellow pencil and answered all the questions I knew. Then I did the ones I sort of knew. I looked at the clock. I only had 15 minutes left to do the hard stuff. All around me I could hear the sound of pencils scratching paper. It made my heart beat fast. I wasn't writing. I was chewing on my pencil so hard I could taste wood.

I took my pencil out of my mouth and stuck out my tongue. I had to curl up the end so I could see the little dots of yellow paint from the outside of the pencil. Yuck! I scrubbed my tongue with the end of my T-shirt, hoping nobody saw. It was sorta gross. But at least the yellow paint came off. I looked at the clock again. Ten minutes left.

In front of me. Trish Riley's hand shot up.

"Yes, Trish?" Mrs. Clay said from her desk at the front of the room.

"There's stuff on here we just had last Friday," Trish complained.

"That's correct," Mrs. Clay replied. "If you were paying attention, it shouldn't be a problem."

Well, it *was* a problem. But then I remembered that I hadn't been listening on Friday when this new stuff came up.

It wasn't really my fault though. It was Muggsy's. He'd chewed up the cuff of Dad's shirt that morning. Dad had been so upset he'd said a bad word. Which made mom get mad at him. Which made the day get off to a rotten start. Who could blame me for worrying about Muggsy's munchies after *that*?

"Five minutes, people," Mrs. Clay warned.

I looked back at my test. Now that I thought about it, it was Sam Sherman's fault even more than Muggsy's. Why hadn't he gone over this new stuff with me? Maybe because he wanted me to fail. Yeah, that was it. He wanted me off the team. He taught me just enough to make himself look good. But not enough to keep me from being kicked off. I looked over at him and scowled. He was done taking his test and was reading his library book.

"Okay. Pencils down," Mrs. Clay ordered. I'd never even picked mine back up. I handed my unfinished paper up to Trish to pass to the front of the room. Then I slumped down in my seat. I was done. Finished. Cooked like a goose.

"So, how did you do on the math test?" Zack asked me at lunch.

"I don't want to talk about it," I answered.

Zack groaned. "That bad, huh? Oh man, Mick."

I didn't answer. There was nothing to say. I'd done the best I could and it wasn't enough. And now I was going to be off the team. A sad picture of me slumped on the bench with the guys who never get to play popped into my head. It made me want to howl. Kick things. Cry even. But I couldn't have a melt-down in the lunchroom with Mrs. Burton on lunch duty. She'd zap me with a detention for sure.

That left the Sam problem to think about. In a way it didn't matter whether I ratted on him. There was nothing he could do to me now. I was already off the team. The thought cheered me up a little. Last night after Zack fell asleep, I'd hatched an idea. It was a little scary. Maybe even dangerous. But I knew I had to do it. Alone. Today.

After school I waited until Zack was on the bus. As soon as it pulled out of the lot and turned the corner I headed for Summer Street.

The big, creepy house loomed like a monster against the dull gray sky. I stood on the broken sidewalk and stared at it. Deep inside on the downstairs floor I could see a light burning. Someone was home. That was good. I could do what I'd come for. But it was also bad because now I had no excuse to wait.

I took a deep breath and started slowly up the walk. In my head I planned what would happen. The owner would open the door. I'd say hi and tell her my name. Then I would ask her if she knew Sam Sherman. If she said no, I'd ask her if she remembered the boy who had handed her the mail that day. I might even ask if she knew who'd broken her back window. I had it all figured out.

The only part I didn't know is what I'd do if she said she *did* know Sam. But there wasn't much chance of that. People from Sam's neighborhood don't hang around with people who live on Summer Street.

Up close the house seemed even spookier than from far away. It had a sad used-up look like a shirt so worn-out you wouldn't even give it to Goodwill.

I took a deep breath and rang the doorbell. A tinny, old-fashioned clang answered from inside the house.

Hi, you don't know me, but my name is Mickey McGhee, I practiced in my head. My heart was pounding so loud I didn't even *need* the doorbell.

Footsteps came toward me from inside. My

heart speeded up. I opened my mouth to give my little speech.

The door swung open. My mouth snapped shut.

I stared.

The person in the doorway stared back.

"Wh-wh-at are *you* doing here?" I stammered.

"The big question is, what are YOU doing here?" he snarled. "You been following me, or what?"

He turned away from the door for a second and spoke to someone inside the house. "It's okay, Jessie," he said. "I've got it."

Jessie? Who was Jessie? And what in the world was Sam Sherman doing in her falling-down house on one of the worst streets in town?

Before I could figure out how to ask, he turned back to me. "Look, I'm busy," he snapped. "You've got no business over here. I told you Sunday that you don't know anything about my life. And you don't. So get lost before I get you thrown off this porch."

He was right. I *didn't* know anything about his life. But I knew what I'd seen and it wasn't good. "Then maybe you better start explaining it to me," I said. The calm, sure sound of my own voice surprised me. "Because if you don't, I'm telling my parents."

Sam's eyes glittered with anger. "I don't have to tell you nothin', Shrimpo," he spat. "Nothin'! Ever! You got that? And you can tell anybody you want whatever you want! See if I care!" The heavy oak door slammed in my face.

For a second I stood on the porch staring at it. If Sam wasn't doing anything wrong, why didn't he just tell me the truth?

Slowly, I turned around and headed across the yard. I stopped under a giant maple tree and looked around. The whole street seemed weighted down, like all the houses were too sad to stand up straight.

I decided to cut through the alley and go home. The faster I got away from Summer Street, the better. All I wanted was to be in my room by myself for awhile. It had been a terrible day.

I trudged home as if weights were tied around my ankles. I tried talking to God about it, but it felt like we had a bad connection. It was probably my own fault. I felt so done-in, I couldn't even pray right.

At home, Meggie yanked open the side door of the house before I was even up the driveway. "Mickey, Zack's looking for you!" she hollered. "He's upstairs. I think he has a secret! I've been waiting and waiting. Where were you?"

"Nowhere," I said, running past her. My heart

picked up speed. Did Zack know something that I didn't?

I raced up two flights of stairs and burst into my room. Zack jumped up off the bed when he saw me. "Mick! Mick!" shouted. "I know who Sam bought the candy for!"

My face fell—*splat*—like a pancake on the floor. *That* was the big secret? Who really cared who Sam bought candy for? That was kid stuff. I had bigger problems to worry about.

Zack didn't seem to notice my lack of excitement. "Yeah," he went on. "He took LaMar back to the store with him. LaMar said he bought a big red satin box of chocolates and they gave him a free gift card. And he wrote Jessica Schultz's name on it."

"Jessica Schultz?" I couldn't help myself. I sort of got interested. "Really? You sure?"

Zack scrunched up his forehead. Suddenly he didn't look quite as certain as before. "Well, I think so," he said. "LaMar said he wrote "Jessie" on the front. Jessica Schultz is the only girl in our class who could be called Jessie. Right?"

Right. But I knew the candy wasn't for Jessica Schultz. Jessica Shultz didn't live on Summer Street.

10

A Change of Heart

"Mickey, may I see you after class?" Mrs. Clay asked the next day.

Tears pricked my eyeballs like needles. I already knew I'd failed the math test. Now I was going to have to listen to her say it. I'd rather have my teeth drilled than hear how I should have studied more. Especially since I *did* study.

Zack flashed me a pity look from the other side of the room. Trish turned around and whispered, "Poor, Mickey."

I slumped down in my seat and ignored them both. I knew they were only trying to be nice. But people feeling sorry for me only made it worse. Nobody, not even Zack, could understand what it felt like to lose basketball.

The whole class rushed past me on their way to lunch. I pretended to be busy sorting valentines.

In nine more hours I'd be in bed and this day would be over. I'd have the "F" in math. I'd be off the team. I'd have a mushy valentine from Trish that would turn my face the color of a heart.

And I'd know who the mysterious Jessie was.

It was probably a stupid idea, but I was going back to Summer Street one last time after school. No matter what Sam did to me, I *had* to find out what was going on.

"Well, Mickey," Mrs. Clay said when we were alone in the room. "I see you don't understand landmarks."

Landmarks were the things I had left blank on the test. They were all about the minimum, the maximum, and something called the mean. All I know about landmarks is they are pretty *mean* stuff. Especially when you don't study them.

"I guess I don't," I mumbled. "Sam and I didn't do that part. But we *did* work for a long time on Sunday. Honest." I stared at my desktop, trying hard to keep the stupid tears in my eyes.

Mrs. Clay nodded. "I can see that," she agreed. "Because you did extremely well on the rest of the test."

My head snapped up. "I did?"

"You did," she said, pulling my test out of the stack on her desk. She came down the aisle and handed it to me. "You didn't miss a single problem on the front. And you only got in trouble about halfway down the back."

I stared at the paper. A giant red C on the front popped out at me.

Mrs. Clay smiled. "Congratulations," she said. "You passed."

I tried to say thanks. But all I could do was stare at her with my mouth hanging open.

"Now this doesn't mean you can sit back and relax," she warned. "You still have to work hard. But I can see that you've made an effort here. I'm proud of you."

I was proud of me too. So proud I could hardly stand it. As soon as she let me go, I walked as fast as I could to the lunch room.

Thank You, God! Thank you, God! Thank you, God! My feet kept time to the words all the way down the hall. I tossed my lunch sack onto the table and just stood there grinning until Zack stopped chewing and looked at me.

"You passed?" he asked. He sounded like he couldn't believe it.

I nodded and grinned wider.

"Way to go, buddy!" he cried, slapping me a high five.

LaMar and Tony hadn't even known I was failing, but they each slapped me a high five too. I looked over at Sam. He was watching us. I knew I should go over and thank him for his help. I even wanted to. But the look on his face kept me at my own table. And kept me worried for the rest of the afternoon.

By the time the Valentine party rolled around, my stomach felt like a pretzel. Not even the pink frosted cupcakes and cherry punch that the room mothers brought in untied it.

Trish turned around eight times to see if I'd opened the valentine from her. I wasn't in the mood for valentines. Especially not a pink one as big as an elephant's foot with my name written in letters the size of the top E on the eye test chart.

All I could think about was the coldness of Sam's glare. And what I still had to do on Summer Street.

As soon as the bell rang, I told Zack to tell Mom I'd be a little late getting home. Then I headed straight for the creepy house. The dark, gloomy weather matched my mood. All my excitement about passing the test was gone. When Sam found out I'd gone back to Summer Street he'd be mad. *Big time* mad.

I took a deep breath and rang the bell. Once again, a clanging sound came from inside. But this time the door jerked open before I was ready. I found myself looking up into the glittering eyes of ... Sam Sherman. *Again*.

"Didn't I tell you to quit following me!" he screamed when he saw it was me. "You've got no right coming back here. Get lost! I mean it, Shrimpo, GET LOST!"

I took a step back. I couldn't believe it. I'd run like an Olympic sprinter and somehow he'd gotten here first. "You should be glad I'm giving you another chance to explain," I said, taking another step back. "I didn't have to. But I appreciate your helping me with math and ..."

"Chance?" Sam spat. "Hah! That's a good one! I don't need any of your chances. This is nobody's business but mine."

"Who's Jessie?" I asked.

The word was like an eraser wiping the sneer off his face. "How do you know about Jessie?" he demanded. His voice was full of bluster, but I could tell he was shocked.

"I have my ways," I answered. "So who is she? Some girl you like?"

"Never mind Jessie," Sam snapped.

"Sammy? Who's there, honey?" a voice called from inside the house.

Sam turned toward it. I took two steps forward and peered into the glass of the narrow window next to the door. An old lady was hobbling toward us. Before Sam could stop her, she was beside him leaning hard on his arm.

"Hello," she said, smiling at me. "You must be a friend of Sammy's."

I gulped and sort of nodded. I didn't have a clue what to do or say.

"Come in. Come," the old lady said, pushing open the rickety wooden screen door. "It's cold out there." She huddled deeper into the huge grey sweater wrapped around her frail body and held the door open for me.

I looked at Sam. His face was as blank as paper. "Thank you, ma'am," I said and stepped into the house past Sam.

It was so dark inside I had to wait for my eyes to get used to the dim light. The house smelled strange like dust, cooked cabbage, and cough syrup all mixed up together. As I glanced around, a sad feeling poured over me. It was the loneliest place I'd ever been to in my life.

"Come into the parlor," the old lady offered. She took my arm and led me into a small room crowded with broken furniture and leaning piles of magazines. "Sammy will boil the water for tea and we'll talk."

Sam flashed me a quick warning. I sat down on the edge of a hard sofa covered with worn green velvet. A split in the material spilled something that looked like hair. Sam headed for the kitchen. On the way he gave me one last glare of warning.

"Oh! What am I thinking of!" the old lady gasped when he was gone. "I don't have much company anymore. Just Sammy mostly, so I'm a little out of practice. But I do have something nice to offer you today." She shuffled over to a cupboard and pulled out a red heart-shaped box.

It was my turn to gasp. LaMar had told Zack that Sam bought a red box of chocolates for somebody named Jessie. Could *this* be Jessie?

"Are—are you Jessie?" I asked, staring at the candy.

The old lady smiled. Her face was creased with so many wrinkles it looked like the lines on my dad's Ohio road map.

"I can see Sammy's been talking about me!" she said, happily. "Did he tell you how I used to take care of him when he was a little boy? Well, I did. When his mama finished law school, she needed somebody to stay with him while she went to work. Of course I was young then—only 75— so I was more than up to the job. From the time he was six months old to the time he was eight, I was with him every day. We're just like this." She held up two crossed fingers.

"You—you, are?" I asked. I could hardly wrap my mind around it.

"That's right," she continued. "I took care of Sammy and now Sammy takes care of me. Look what he brought me for Valentine's Day." She lifted the lid on the candy box and held out an unbroken heart of chocolates.

"Go on, take one," she urged.

I reached in and took a chocolate-covered caramel. But I didn't eat it. I held it between my fingers and tried to find the words to say what I needed to say.

"I didn't know that, ma'am," I said, looking toward the kitchen. Sam was busy running water, but he'd be back soon. "I thought ... well, the thing is ..." I stammered. "I thought I saw Sam steal your mail and break into your house and fool around in your trash."

"And you thought he was doing something wrong?" the old lady finished for me. She set the candy box on a table and sank into a chair.

"Oh, my goodness, no. That's not the way it is at all! Sammy is so good to me. The only mail he ever takes away is those prize things. Sometimes I spend too much money on magazines hoping to win the jackpot. I'm just greedy, I guess." She laughed a little at that. "Sammy takes them away so I won't be tempted. It's all right though. I told him to."

"But he broke your window ..." I argued. I couldn't believe what this woman named Jessie was saying. The person she was talking about couldn't be the same Sam Sherman who made my life miserable.

Jessie nodded. "Yes, I know that day," she said. "I had washed my kitchen floor. It's so hard for me to keep things clean anymore. But I mopped the floor—and then what did I do? Turned right around and slipped on it. Sammy knocked and when I didn't answer he came through the window. He helped me up, saw I was okay, settled me on the couch, and made me a cup of tea. He even got his mama to get me new glass for the window."

She chuckled and leaned forward. "I'll bet that took some doing! Just between you, me, and the fence post, that woman can be tight with the dollar! As for that trash, I bet that's the day he was looking for my false teeth!"

I sat on the edge of the hard sofa and let my brain sift through this amazing news. Mom had been right after all. Sam Sherman *had* done something *good*. I thought about what he did for Jessie and how he'd helped me with math. Then I decided something.

"I better be going now, ma'am," I said, standing up. "Thanks for the candy and for talking to me about this and everything. Could I—uh—ask you a favor?"

"What's that?" Jessie asked.

"Could you tell Sam thanks for me?" I said. "Tell him that his secret's safe. He'll understand."

If Sam didn't want anybody to know he had a good side that was okay with me. What mattered was that he had taken time to do something *nice* for someone else, and that I'd taken the time to find it out. He could go on being a tough guy forever if that's what he wanted. And he wanted it. I knew it. Just like I knew he'd go on making me just as miserable as he always does.

I didn't wait for Jessie to answer. I ran out the door into the cold February air. I'd just realized something so huge it boggled my mind. Jesus had forgiven the people who'd hung Him on the cross! If He could do something that hard, I knew He could help me forgive Sam Sherman for calling me Shrimpo. As I ran toward home I asked Him to help me do it. I knew it wouldn't be easy, but somehow I had to begin.

By the time I reached Wooster Street, I'd changed my mind about Valentine's Day. At the corner I dropped my backpack on the sidewalk and squatted down beside it. There was something I suddenly wanted to read. I reached in and pulled out the big pink envelope the size of an elephant's foot.

On the front of the card a cheerleader waved her pompons and did the splits in the air. Inside, it said, "Three cheers for you, Valentine! From Trish." The only mushy thing about it was the tiny heart dotting the "i."

But wait! There was something else. I turned

over a piece of paper. It looked like an award with a gold sticker pasted on the front.

It said,

Not tran-fer-able. Valid for life

"THIS SIR-TIFF-IKIT ENTITLES

the bearer (that's you, MICKEY!)
and his dog, Muggsy,

to FREE obedience school lessons
taught by Patricia Ann Riley.

These lessons will last however long it takes to get
Muggsy over the munchies.

Not tran-fer-able. Valid for life."

I couldn't help it. I laughed right out loud. Sometimes that Trish Riley cracks me up!